The Racing WORM Brothers

Story • Gary Barwin   Art • Kitty Macaulay

Annick Press • Toronto • New York

THE CANADA COUNCIL   LE CONSEIL DES ARTS
FOR THE ARTS   DU CANADA
SINCE 1957   DEPUIS 1957

We acknowledge the support of the Canada Council
for the Arts for our publishing program.
We also thank the Ontario Arts Council.

Cataloguing in Publication Data

Barwin, Gary
    The racing worm brothers

ISBN 1-55037-541-5 (bound) ISBN 1-55037-540-7 (pbk.)

I. Macaulay, Kitty. II. Title.

PS8553.A783R32 1998   jC813'.54   C98-930314-4
PZ7.B37Ra 1998

The art in this book was rendered in watercolours.
The text was typeset in Quill Script.

Distributed in Canada by:
Firefly Books Ltd.
3680 Victoria Park Avenue
Willowdale, ON
M2H 3K1

Published in the U.S.A. by Annick Press (U.S.) Ltd.
Distributed in the U.S.A. by:
Firefly Books (U.S.) Inc.
P.O. Box 1338
Ellicott Station
Buffalo, NY 14205

Printed and bound in Canada by Friesens.

FOR THE WHOLE WORM FAMILY
G.B.

FOR MICHEL AND NICOLAS
K.M.

A goldfish was the only pet that Aaron was allowed. Any other pet would sneeze and break out in bumps because Aaron was allergic.

Aaron put his hand in the fish tank.

"Stop!" his brother Ryan said. "You can't pat a goldfish!"

"But I want a pet that I can touch."

"Then let's get some worms," Ryan said. "Worms love being patted."

Ryan found a long and skinny worm at the back of the yard.
Aaron found a short, fat one near the fence.

"My worm is called Pinky," Ryan said.

"Mine's called Worm," Aaron said. "And he likes to be patted."

Ryan said, "I think our worms are brothers."

Aaron said, "Our worm brothers look tired."

The boys held their worms close and sang a worm song.

"Look at our sweet little worms," Ryan whispered. "They've gone to sleep." The brothers tucked the worms into tissue-paper beds for a nap.

After a few minutes Aaron said, "Time to wake up, Worm," and Ryan said, "Wakey, wakey, Pinky-winky." They put the worms on the swings for a ride. Pinky liked swinging high and fast, but Worm got scared and wanted to get off.

"Let's take him for a ride on my tricycle," Aaron said.
"Worm wants to look around. And he likes the wind blowing
through his hair."

"Worms don't have hair," Ryan said.

"Worm has hair—he just had a haircut and it's very
short. And he likes me to brush it," Aaron said, "—with my
toothbrush."

Ryan explained to Pinky about reading. Worm had never been to school but Aaron told him, "Don't be afraid, brave little worm," and showed him how to count to ten.

Then Ryan suggested that they have a worm race. He drew a starting line near the swings. The finish line was the stop sign at the very end of the street.

When the worms were ready, Ryan shouted, "Go!" and the worm race began.

They ran to the end of the street to wait for the worms.

Ryan said, "Pinky is the world's fastest worm. Your worm is slow as spaghetti."

"My worm is going to win," Aaron said. "GO, WORM!" he shouted.

They waited for a long time at the finish line, but the
worms didn't come. They ran back along the racecourse,
looking for their worms.

"Worms!" Aaron called. "Where are you?"

"Here, Pinky! Here, Worm!" Ryan called, but they couldn't
find their worms anywhere.

"I know," Ryan said. "They've gone into the dirt. They have their own world underground."

"Worms like to *race* underground," Aaron said.

"They're going to crawl under everyone's yard until they get to the finish line," Ryan said.

"How will they know where to go?"

"We'll draw them a map."

The worm map was filled with squiggly lines showing the worms how to dig through the neighbourhood. There were squares showing each backyard and each house.

Other important things were marked on the map: Ryan and Aaron's playhouse, Jamie and Meg's sandbox, Kiera's climbing-tree.

The boys put the map near the fence. "They'll come up at night to see the map," Ryan explained.

It was Aaron's idea to make places for the worms to rest along the way. He made more tissue-paper beds and put them into old yogurt containers, which he left at different places along the racecourse.

At supper Ryan said, "Pinky will be the first to wiggle out of our yard."

"No, Worm already crawled under the fence," Aaron said. "He took one look at the map and started squiggling like crazy."

In bed that night, Ryan and Aaron imagined Pinky and Worm crawling under the grass of their neighbours' yard. They imagined the worms having a rest in their tissue-paper beds.

Then the worms would look at the map in the moonlight.

"Try and catch me," Pinky would say to Worm. "I'm the fastest worm in the world!"

"But I crawled under the fence first," Worm said, and started wiggling to catch up with Pinky.

The next morning, the boys moved the map to Jamie and Meg's yard.

Each day for the rest of the summer, the boys put their ears to the ground listening for the worms.

"I can hear Worm," Aaron said. "He's winning."

"Pinky hasn't been trying," Ryan said. "He's going to start really racing in a minute."

And each morning the boys moved the map. One day it was beside Kiera's climbing-tree, the next day it was in Mrs. Ehlert's flower garden.

During the day the boys drew sidewalk chalk-pictures of the world's longest worm.

They pretended there were worms in their spaghetti.

They lay down in the grass and told stories to their worms underground.

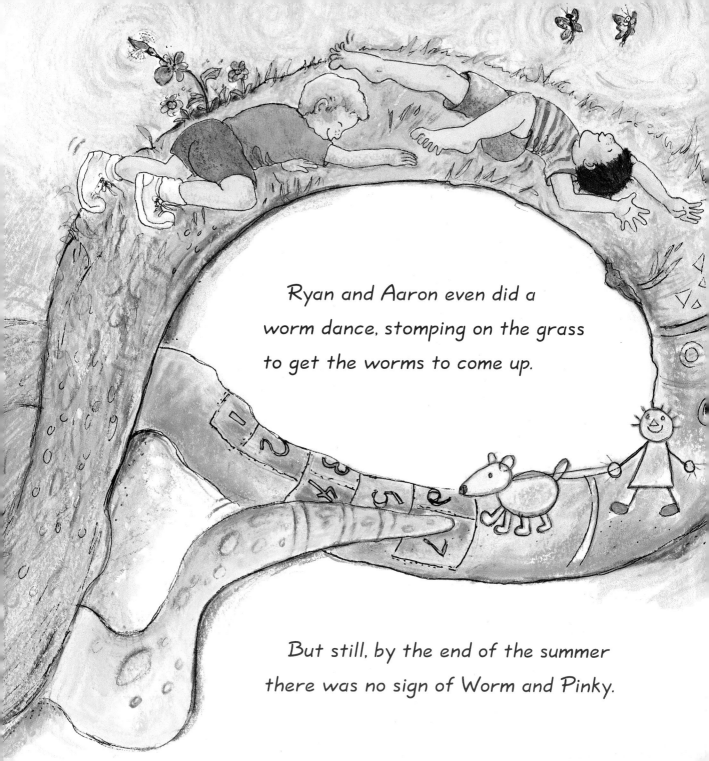

Ryan and Aaron even did a worm dance, stomping on the grass to get the worms to come up.

But still, by the end of the summer there was no sign of Worm and Pinky.

It was raining on the morning of the first day of school. There were puddles everywhere. Ryan and Aaron did one more worm dance. But there was still no sign of them.

The boys walked down the street toward the school, past Jamie and Meg's, past Kiera's, past Mrs. Ehlert's and past Mrs. Johnson's big, black dog barking through the fence. They were standing at the stop sign, waiting for a car to drive by, when Aaron noticed something pink on the edge of the sidewalk.

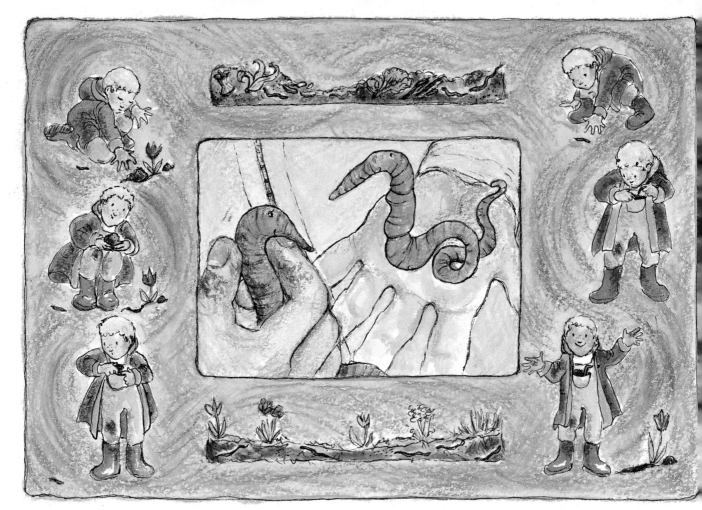

"WORM!" Aaron shouted, picking up a short, fat worm. "You came back!"

"PINKY!" Ryan yelled, picking up a long, skinny worm. "You finished the race."

The worm brothers wouldn't tell which one had finished the race first.

"Pinky isn't braggy," Ryan said.

"No, Worm doesn't want Pinky to feel bad," said Aaron, walking into the schoolyard.

There were five hundred children on the first day of school. Some brought pencils. Some brought balls. Some brought snacks in their backpacks. Only two brought their pets in their pockets.

And it seemed to Ryan and Aaron that the worms liked their teachers...

...better than the teachers liked their worms.